MICROSAURS

THAT'S MY TINY-SAURUS REX

MICROSAURS

THAT'S MY TINY-SAURUS REX

DUSTIN HANSEN

Feiwel and Friends
New York

A FEIWEL AND FRIENDS BOOK
An imprint of Macmillan Publishing Group, LLC
175 Fifth Avenue, New York, NY 10010

MICROSAURS: THAT'S MY TINY-SAURUS REX. Copyright © 2018 by Dustin Hansen.
All rights reserved. Printed in the United States of America by
LSC Communications, Harrisonburg, Virginia.

Our books may be purchased in bulk for promotional, educational,
or business use. Please contact your local bookseller or the Macmillan
Corporate and Premium Sales Department at (800) 221-7945 ext. 5442
or by e-mail at MacmillanSpecialMarkets@macmillan.com.

Library of Congress Control Number: 2017944814

ISBN 978-1-250-09029-4 (hardcover) / ISBN 978-1-250-09031-7 (ebook)

Book design by Liz Dresner
Feiwel and Friends logo designed by Filomena Tuosto

First edition, 2018

10 9 8 7 6 5 4 3 2 1

mackids.com

For Annie and Sam,

The two best friends I've ever seen

L in chewed, swallowed, then opened her mouth and stuck out her tongue. Specks and crumbs from Fruity Stars cereal covered it like glitter.

"Five minutes and eleven seconds. I'm not sure it's a world record, but I'm impressed," I said to Lin as I checked my stopwatch.

"I bet it is a world record. How do we find out?" Lin asked as she dusted cereal crumbs off the front of her shirt. "Should we call the Fruity Stars cereal company? I bet they'd know."

"We'll write down the time and call them later. Right now, we need to turn that box into a new lab for the Microterium. Remember?" I said. I held out my hand for Lin to pass me the box.

"Of course I remember. I just think that setting a world record for fastest time ever for eating a whole box of cereal, *without milk even*, is something pretty special," Lin said. She handed me the box.

"Absolutely. And I promise we'll look into it. But for now, it's construction time," I said as I placed the box on the kitchen table. "Marker."

Lin dug through my backpack and found a blue marker. She handed it to me. "My lips are all chappy and my cheeks are sore on the insides of my mouth."

I measured the center of the box and drew a square where I would be cutting a hole for the front door to the new Fruity Stars Lab. "Hazards of the job, I guess," I said. "Scissors."

Lin pulled a pair of scissors from the caddy on the table and handed them to me, handles first. Not only is Lin an excellent cereal muncher, she is the best lab assistant I've ever met. I used the scissors to cut a perfectly straight door hole, then I bent it open, creasing a hinge in the cardboard so it would open and shut.

"Will you please hand me that masking tape?" I said to Lin.

"Thure . . ." Lin said. I looked at her to see her tongue was lolling out of her mouth. "My thongue ith sthwollen up. Ith thath mormal?"

I laughed—I couldn't help it—which made Lin a little angry. "I'm theriouth, Danny. It'th puffing up like a balloon," Lin said. Lin pinched her tongue and held it out as far as she could, trying to see it over her nose.

I reached for the tape myself. "I'm sure you'll be fine. Your tongue just did a big workout session. It probably needs a rest. Maybe have a glass of milk or something," I said.

"Thath'th a good ithea," Lin said. It made me laugh again and I kind of put the tape on crooked, but it was fine. Hearing Lin talk with her tongue hanging out of her mouth was totally worth a crooked piece of tape.

I could hear Lin digging through the fridge as I added a few more details to the Fruity Stars cereal box. I cut two windows in the top of the box to let in some light. Then I pinched the top of the roof into a triangle, like Professor Penrod had done with the first cereal box. The original held up fine for a while, but after Lin and I introduced a few rowdy Microsaurs to the Microterium, the box was pretty much destroyed.

"The milk helpths, but I think thith thrawberry thoda will be even better," Lin said. She leaned around the fridge door and showed me a half-empty bottle of red, sugary soda.

"Thure thing. Thelp thourthelf," I said.

"Ha-ha, very thunny, Danny," Lin said. She unscrewed the cap and drank right from the bottle.

Just then, my phone started to buzz and beep. Looking around, I dug under papers until I found it buried beneath the plans I'd drawn earlier for the new lab. A notification had popped up, and I swiped the screen to check it out.

"Looks like we have exactly four hours and fifty-three minutes until Professor Penrod returns," I said.

"That's *tons* of time," Lin said. She put the bottle back in the fridge. "And hey, look. I'm cured! Strawberry soda to the rescue!"

I had a feeling Lin had waited her whole life to shout that. "Tons of time for what?" I asked.

"To go to the zoo," Lin said.

"The zoo?" I asked. "Don't you mean the Microterium?"

"Sure, but the zoo, too. Remember? It's the last day of Junior Zookeeper's Class. And it's only the most important day. We're talking about FOOD, and I want to show my Microbites to Annie and Sam. I bet they will want to buy my recipe to feed to their animals. Hey. Maybe even other humans, too. They are pretty good," Lin said.

"I have to agree, I'm kind of addicted to them. Especially when you add raisins," I said.

"I always add raisins," Lin said. "Everyone knows triceratops love raisins."

"Well, how about this? We stop by the Microterium first. We remove what's left of the old Fruity Stars Lab and replace it with this masterpiece," I said as I showed the completed cereal box lab to Lin.

"Awesome. The Fruity Stars Lab, Part Two: The Reckoning," Lin said, and I tilted my head.

"The what?" I asked.

"Oh, nothing. It was a scary movie I saw once. I don't even know what it means, but it sounds good," Lin said.

"We'll keep working on it," I said. "Besides, we need to check on Pizza and Cornelia. Last night was their first night alone in the Microterium." Since they hatched, they've been staying with one of us in the mint case at night. "It was a big night for them, and I wanna make sure they are okay."

"For sure. I'll grab them some snacks, too," Lin said.

I started stuffing things in my backpack as Lin grabbed her Microbites and some pepperoni slices, and chunked up some corn-dog parts for the Microsaurs. Once my pack was all stuffed and Lin's pockets were crammed with plastic bags full of snacks, I checked Professor Penrod's progress on my phone one more time.

"Four hours, forty-four minutes, and forty-four seconds," I said.

"No way! That's gotta be lucky, right?" Lin said.

"I don't really think numbers are lucky," I said.

"Well, they can be. And that many fours all strung together has got to be lucky," Lin said as she snapped the strap of her skateboard helmet under her chin. "It's gonna be a good day, Danny."

"The best," I said as we tied the box containing the Fruity Stars Lab 2.0 onto Lin's skateboard using a bungee cord we found in my garage. Then we push-pulled it as fast as we could toward the greatest place on earth—Professor Penrod's supersecret, hidden-away, tiny-dinosaur-filled Microterium.

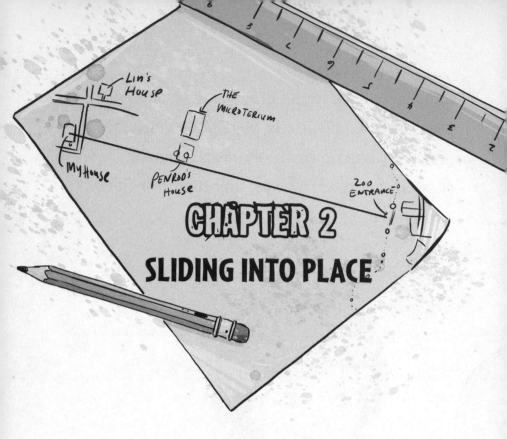

CHAPTER 2
SLIDING INTO PLACE

I f you take a map of our town and use a ruler to draw a straight line from my house to the zoo, your pencil would go right through the Microterium.

Despite her added package, Lin made it to Penrod's first, squeezing through the iron gate that surrounded the house. I chased after her, the tall grass of the backyard tickling my legs as I ran toward the old barn that contained the professor's lab.

"This shouldn't take long," I said to Lin as she threw the door open.

Blinking, we paused to let our eyes adjust. The professor's barn-lab was dark inside. Come to think of it, it was more of a collector's room than an actual laboratory, which were usually bright so you don't miss any of the science. Dinosaur bones, old books, and chemistry supplies were scattered about, and photos of Professor Penrod's adventures were tucked all around in tiny frames he made himself. But the real magic of the barn-lab was hidden behind a picture of his childhood dog. If you didn't know the secret, you'd never guess that with one simple twist, the whole wall lowers into the floor, revealing the Microterium.

"That never gets old," I said as I laid my eyes on the Microterium. Large glass windows in the roof of the barn let in plenty of sunlight, and Professor Penrod had designed the place so perfectly it looked like the world's greatest science fair diorama.

"Totally," Lin said, then she took three big steps into the Microterium itself, heading toward the destroyed Fruity Stars Lab.

"Be careful," I warned, even though I knew that was a silly thing to say. Sure, Lin was the type of girl who would jump off a two-story building onto an old slippery slide while riding a skateboard and juggling three wild kittens, but she was also the type of person who could tiptoe around in a dense garden of leaves and grass without harming a single flea. Or, in our case, a single Microsaur.

"So, this place is a pretty big mess inside, too," Lin said as she stood up holding what was left of the old lab in her hands. "It looks like everything is scattered around and all messed up. There are teeny-tiny books everywhere."

"Oh boy. I had a feeling that would happen," I said. Being the tiny descendants of ancient dinosaurs that once ruled the planet didn't really prepare the Microsaurs for being neat and tidy. Holding the new Fruity Stars cereal box, I took three careful steps toward Lin to inspect the mess. "You're right. It looks like your bedroom."

"It's not *that* bad," Lin said, and we both laughed. We both knew her bedroom was a natural disaster.

I carefully placed the new cereal box right where the old box had been. I didn't want to accidentally smash any of Professor Penrod's equipment. Especially the Expand-O-Matic! The machine the professor had invented to unshrink you after a visit into the Microterium seemed sturdy and big when you were the size of a Microsaur, but now that Lin and I were normal-sized it looked *super* fragile.

"So, now what? Do you have tweezers or something that we can use to put all the stuff back in the new lab?" Lin asked. "Or are we gonna shrink down and do it? And, I don't know, maybe play with the Microsaurs for a few minutes while we're at it?"

I looked at Lin and gave her a crooked smile. "Uh, yeah, we're going to shrink down. Of course."

"Yes! I knew it!" Lin nearly flew back to the barn, leaving me alone in the Microterium. "Shrinking is my favorite part," she said. "Well, riding Zip-Zap is my *actual* favorite, but you have to be little to do that, so yeah. It's all my favorite, I guess."

"Well, I think I have something new that will be your favorite part," I said.

"Really, what is it? Are we going to ride Pizza and Cornelia?" Lin asked.

"Nope," I said. I pulled off my backpack and set it on the floor.

"Are we going to go swimming with Honk-Honk again? That was pretty amazing," Lin said.

"It was amazing, but I'm not so sure I want to wear soggy clothes to the zoo. Besides, this is even better," I said as I removed something new from my backpack.

"Are we going to fly with Twiggy again? Get chased by Bruno? What, tell me!" Lin said.

"We're going to try out my new invention, the Slide-A-Riffic." I showed my new contraption to Lin.

It was simple in concept—basically just sliding down a string—but I'd had to really think about how to make it work. The basket

that would hold Lin and me was made from an old chewable vitamins bottle that I'd carved down to be just the right size. I'd looped two used guitar strings through a system of gears and pulleys I had connected to the vitamin bottle with my Plastic Interlocking Building Blocks, PIBBs for short, a new interlocking block system my dad and I were inventing. And finally, I wrapped the strings around two old toothbrushes I wasn't using anymore, then hammered the toothbrushes deep into the soil to hold things in place. All in all, I was darned proud of the new invention, and I couldn't wait to try it out.

"What does it do?" Lin asked.

"Well, you know how it only takes three steps to get to the Fruity Stars Lab when we're big?" I asked.

"Sure," Lin said, her eyes getting wide.

"And it takes like an hour to climb over the

hills and mountains when we are tiny-sized, right?" I said.

"Yeah. Even if we get rides from the Microsaurs it takes a long time. Go on. I'm listening," Lin said.

"Well, now that I have this pulley system down by the Fruity Stars Lab, all I have to do is hook this transit retaining arm to the big metal step in the barn, and . . ." I said before Lin broke in.

"And then we climb in the little white tub thingy and zip on these metal strings all the way down to the lab in like half a second," Lin said. Her eyes were so wide I thought she might pop.

"Well, if my calculations are correct, it'll be more like thirty seconds, but still, it'll be fast and easy," I said.

"Oh my GOSH! Hook it up, Danny. Let's give it a try. You put your new Slide-A-Riffic in place, and we'll meet on the metal step! GO!" Lin said.

I double-checked to make sure everything

was set up nice and secure, then looked up to see that Lin was already standing on the metal step that worked like an on switch, sending the shrinking potion through a series of tubes and out the spray nozzle above. I jumped onto the metal step, joining Lin, and our combined weight was enough to start the process. In no time at all we were the size of ants, running toward the new Slide-A-Riffic.

I climbed in first, then gave Lin a hand to pull her inside the basket with me.

"It smells like vitamins," Lin said, taking a big sniff. "I like that a lot!"

"It's a feature," I said with a smile. Then, putting on my best announcer voice, I said, "Welcome, Slide-A-Riffic riders of all ages. Please keep your arms and legs inside the vehicle at all times. Hold tight and enjoy your ride. Ready?"

Lin nodded, and I wrapped my hands around a blue plastic lever and gave it a yank to release the Slide-A-Riffic.

Lin raised her hands over her head and started to shout as the slide began to roll.

I think she was expecting a faster ride, because we hadn't moved hardly at all before she lowered her hands and turned back to me with a quizzical look on her face. "Is this as fast as it's going to go?" she asked.

I shrugged, totally happy with the speed we were moving. There was a nice breeze, and the view was amazing as we soared along high in the air.

"Okay. It's slow, but it's still awesome," Lin said.

"This is my idea of riding in style," I said, but as we slid farther away from the step, the little plastic pulley wheels started rolling faster and faster. With every inch of the guitar string that we traveled, the Slide-A-Riffic picked up speed, which was totally not what I had planned. "Um, Lin. I think I forgot something," I admitted.

"What?" Lin said. She was hanging out over the front of the basket, her arms stretched out as if she were trying to take flight.

"Brakes!" I shouted as the Slide-A-Riffic began zooming toward the ground.

"Yeeeeeee-haaaaah!" Lin shouted at the very tip-top of her adventure-seeking voice.

As we zoomed over the hill, the Slide-A-Riffic basket swayed as it brushed against the tops of the trees. We picked up more momentum and we barely slowed down as we burst through branches, knocking leaves and twigs in every

direction. We popped out of the little grove of trees, and I braced for impact.

The bottom of the Slide-A-Riffic crashed into the soft earth of the Microterium, leaving behind a dark scar of mud beneath the grass. We bounced back up, and for a quiet moment I heard nothing but the air rushing by again. Then we slammed to the ground again. Lin and I were both thrown from the basket, and we rolled over and over until we tumbled to a stop.

"That was . . ." I started, then Lin took over.

"The most amazing Slide-A-Riffic ride in the history of the world!" Lin jumped up.

"Also . . . the first. And probably the last," I said. My hand went to the back of my head. I found a lump as big as a robin's egg, and my rear end felt like I had landed on a rock the size of a grapefruit.

I checked. I had.

"Are you kidding me? We're going to do it again right now," Lin said. "This time you ride in front. It is a *much* better view up front."

"Uh, the answer you're looking for is somewhere between 'no thanks' and 'never again as long as I live,'" I said. "Besides, we have a lot to do today. We'll try it again as soon as I can figure out a braking system. What was I thinking?"

"All right, but I get to control the brakes," Lin said.

"Yeah, that's not going to happen, either," I said as I stood up and dusted off my pants.

The sun was shining down on the brightly colored cereal box as Lin pointed to the new lab. "It looks pretty good. Professor Penrod will be surprised."

The new Fruity Stars Lab cereal box didn't just look good, it looked great. It was nice to see it without any holes in it—except the ones that were *supposed* to be there, of course.

"Let's go check it out," I said.

Lin and I ran inside the new Fruity Stars Lab 2.0 and took a look around.

"Well, it's not as bad as I thought it would be when we were big," I said. "It won't take us very long at all to straighten things out."

"I told you it was our lucky day, Danny. We didn't get hurt after you forgot the Slide-A-Riffic brakes, we have tons of time before Penny returns, and the inside of the new lab isn't even close to as messy as my room," Lin said.

"You can say that again," I said. "How about this? You start stacking Professor Penrod's books back on this shelf and I'll look around for something to use for brakes for the Slide-A-Riffic."

"Good idea. Unless . . ." Lin said. She rubbed her chin with her thumb and forefinger, just like I did when I was trying to think really hard. She picked up two large, leather-covered books. "Unless you can use these as brakes."

"Yeah, I'm not so sure using Professor Penrod's book collection to stop the Slide-A-Riffic is the best idea. You work on stacking, and I'll work on stopping. Deal?" I said.

"Deal," Lin said as she began filling the bookshelf.

I rummaged through Professor Penrod's equipment, looking for something to stop the

Slide-A-Riffic. I found some rubber bands that might work, some half-chewed-up pencil erasers that had promise, and a bottle of rubber cement that might have the right amount of goo, but nothing was quite right. I was lost in deep thought when Lin spoke.

"Hey. Isn't this Professor Penrod's guidebook thingy?" Lin said. She was holding an old notebook with a dinosaur print stamped into its leather cover.

"Yeah. That's it. Can I see it, please? Maybe there's something in there about stopping a runaway Slide-A-Riffic."

"Sure, but you're probably more likely to find something about stopping a runaway triceratops," Lin said as she slid the book over to me on the top of a dice that Professor Penrod used as a lab table. "Where do you think Pizza and Cornelia are? Don't you think it's kind of strange we haven't seen any Microsaurs since we've been here?"

With all the excitement of nearly crashing the Slide-A-Riffic and installing the new Fruity Stars Lab 2.0, I hadn't really thought about it, but Lin was right.

"Yeah, actually. That is odd," I said. The rubber end of a suction cup dart poked up from beneath a stack of fallen papers, and I thought I might have an idea of how to fix the braking problem.

"How 'bout you call for them while I see if I can turn this dart into some kind of braking system?"

Lin didn't need me to suggest again. She ran from the new lab and started shouting for the Microsaurs. "Cornelia. Pizza. Zip-Zap. Where are you?"

After stuffing a broken pencil inside the foam end of the dart, I grabbed a couple of rubber bands and started dragging my new parts toward the Slide-A-Riffic. From the woods, I noticed a strange sound, kind of like a big, rumbling tummy. But it was far off and I'd heard stranger sounds in the Microterium, so I didn't give it much thought.

Beneath a stack of blueprint drawings, Lin found Professor Penrod's trumpet. It was a little dented, but that didn't stop Lin.

BRRRRRAAAAP! Lin tooted on the horn.

"Honk-Honk! Where are you?" Lin shouted, then she tooted the horn again. Usually Honk-Honk came running in at once when she heard the horn, but this time she was nowhere to be seen.

I was about to start wrapping the rubber band around my new brake system when I heard Lin make a huge snort.

"Ha. Nice one, Lin," I shouted over my shoulder. I secured the rubber-band-and–foam-dart braking system in place. It wasn't perfect, but it would work.

"What? I thought it was you," Lin said.

The snort rumbled again, but this time I was looking right at Lin. I could tell it wasn't her at all. It almost sounded like a growl. It was coming from the thick woods to the right of the new Fruity Stars Lab 2.0.

"That wasn't a snort. Was that Cornelia?" Lin said. Then a second growl echoed from the left.

"That can't be Pizza," I said. "The sound was . . . I don't know. Too big. Too grown-up."

Lin and I stopped what we were doing and started scanning around for the twin baby tiny-saurus rexes. The twins had only hatched a few days ago, but they had already had plenty of practice creating problems before they were even hatched.

Then a welcome sight popped out of the woods. "Zip-Zap!" Lin shouted as she ran toward the fastest, most beautifully colored Microsaur ever.

Lin tossed her arms around the big, birdlike Microsaur, but that didn't stop Zip-Zap from bouncing around. He shook his feathery wings and tilted his head back and forth nervously. His long toes were scratching in the dirt, carving tracks in the ground.

"What's wrong, boy?" Lin asked, but even her most soothing tones didn't calm Zip-Zap.

The growl returned, but this time it was joined by a rumbling, tumbling noise that sounded like distant thunder. Zip-Zap pulled away from Lin, turned around, and dipped his head toward the sound. He puffed up all his feathers and squinted his eyes down like he was ready for a fight. For such a silly and fun-loving Microsaur, Zip-Zap can really look terrifying if he needs to.

"Look, over there," Lin said, pointing in the direction Zip-Zap was staring. A cloud of dust rose above the puffy trees behind the Fruity Stars Lab.

"I don't like the looks of that," I said. The noise grew louder and clearer. Now we could hear clicking and screeching and thumping. "Or the sound of it, for that matter."

CHAPTER 4
TERRIBLE TWIN TROUBLE

A bright blue mass burst from the forest first. His three greenish horns tore through the woods like he was pushing through blades of grass, not sturdy tree trunks. Bruno was clearly running away from something, his eyes open wide, his big mouth pulled down at the corners, running as fast as he could . . . straight for the new Fruity Stars Lab!

Zip-Zap gave up his brave pose and shot straight in the air when he saw Bruno charging, which jolted Lin and me into action as well. We turned and sprinted toward the lab, trying to head off the fleeing Microsaurs.

"Oh no, this is going to be bad," Lin said.

The first of the oviraptors burst from the trees, following along in the path that Bruno had carved with his massive, bony head.

"They are going to destroy the lab again!" I shouted.

Five or six more oviraptors shot from the woods. Honestly, with all the chaos it was hard to keep count. They ran in a wild pack toward Zip-Zap, who had landed halfway up our freshly rebuilt lab, perching nervously in a window I'd cut in the box less than an hour before.

The oviraptors scattered, running around the base of the lab and making a dust cloud. A few of them tried to scratch and scurry their way up the box in hopes of reaching Zip-Zap. The cardboard sagged where the Microsaurs crowded around, and I was afraid they were going to tear right through.

"Get down from there!" Lin shouted, but she might as well have shouted her address, the words to "Yankee-Doodle-Dandy," and a recipe for tofu soup, because the Microsaurs did not listen. And they certainly did not *obey*!

The entire pack of tiny-raptors had joined the mess. Then we finally saw the cause of all this commotion. Right behind them, with silly grins on their toothy mouths, were the youngest members of the Microterium. The trouble-causing, Microsaur-chasing, always-hungry Pizza and Cornelia.

Zip-Zap started to lose his balance. He jumped from his window perch, flapping his flightless wings for balance as he headed for the top of the Fruity Stars Lab. He reached out with his pointy claws to get a better grip, but instead he started to slip down the face of the cereal box. As he skittered down, he left behind six long cuts in the front of the lab.

Meanwhile, probably looking for a place to hide, four of the oviraptors had run inside the Fruity Stars Lab. Clanging sounds rang in my ears, and I winced as I imagined the mess they were creating.

"Quick. In the lab!" I shouted, and Lin followed me inside after the tiny-raptors.

One of them was standing on the desk, looking nervous and jumpy, its eyes twitching and blinking. It kicked off a large round glass beaker, and I had to dive to catch it before it crashed to the floor.

"Shoo them out of here, Lin!"

Lin grabbed the lid of the trash can and a pair of metal tongs. She started clanging the two together and shouting at the overexcited Microsaurs. "Get out of here, you mess makers!" Lin shouted.

Two ran out, but I could hear Pizza and Cornelia growling and howling outside the lab, and six more tiny-raptors ran in. Zip-Zap was still trying to scratch his way to safety on top of the lab, but he was only slicing it to shreds.

I ran around the lab, catching books, a keyboard, a pair of Penrod's spare reading glasses, and a fossilized print of a stegosaurus. My arms were so full I was about to topple over when things got worse.

Not bothering to use the door, Bruno smashed his way through the wall of the Fruity Stars Lab. He used his thick skull to bounce the tiny-raptors right out of the lab, one by one. A few of them went through the front door, but most of them were blasted through the cardboard walls of the lab. Bruno must have sensed that Lin and I were in trouble. It's usually a good quality to have. I mean, who doesn't love having a friend that will come to your rescue when times are tough? But while his bravery was appreciated, his methods were not. By the time Bruno was finished clearing them out, the walls looked like Swiss cheese.

He sat down right in the middle of the lab, grinned at his job well done, then licked my face with his massive pink tongue. I rubbed his nose-horn, and he woofed.

"Good boy, Bruno," was all I could say. After all, his heart was in the right place. It's just that his feet, horns, and massive tail are bigger than his heart.

Pizza and Cornelia continued their chase, spooking the pack of tiny-raptors away and disappearing back into the forest from where they had arrived less than two disastrous minutes before.

Lin was trying to convince Zip-Zap to come down as shreds of cardboard floated down from above. The Popsicle sticks we'd used to help prop up the walls and make a small fence around the

Fruity Stars Lab were nothing more than slivers. Books were once again scattered all around, and the lab tables were toppled over.

"This is an epic disaster," I said.

"There's got to be something more than epic. Jumbo? Whopping?" Lin suggested as we looked around at the mess.

"Colossal? Astronomical?" I added.

"Mammoth," Lin said, and we both nodded.

"Yup. That's it. This is a mammoth disaster," I said.

Zip-Zap ducked beneath a broken pencil that we'd used as a main support for the center of the Fruity Stars Lab and joined us in the mess. "Hey, Zippy. Want to help us fix this?" Lin asked.

"I don't think we can," I said, looking around at the destruction. "We're going to have to start from scratch."

"There's a problem with that, actually," Lin said.

"What's that?" I asked.

"If I have to eat one more Fruity Star, I'm going to turn into a fruity solar system," she said.

"That's okay," I replied. "It's obvious cardboard is NOT Microsaur-proof, and we need to come up with a plan for the twins before rebuilding anyway. They're barely hatched and they are already causing huge problems."

"Mammoth problems," Lin said, and I shook my head in agreement.

We sat there, the four of us, and we all thought to ourselves about ways we could rebuild the new lab. Honestly, Bruno and Zip-Zap weren't a lot of help, but Lin and I discussed materials we could use that might be Microsaur-proof. Everything from a metal cake pan to a fish tank. Nothing seemed just right. I took off my backpack and slumped it to the ground next to me and I heard something clink around in the bottom of my bag. Something that might be the answer to our problems.

"Hey, I know what we could try," I said. "And I actually have some with me right now. I brought along a few extra just in case the Slide-A-Riffic needed a repair."

Excited by my new idea, I dug to the very bottom and found a handful of brightly colored PIBBs. "These might do the trick," I said as I showed them to Lin.

"It'll take us three hundred years to build something as big as a lab with PIBBs. And it'll take about a bazillion of the little bricks to do the job," Lin said.

"It would . . . if they were little," I said as I picked my way through the mess toward the Expand-O-Matic. "But even if it does take three hundred years, a test is probably a good idea before we spend the time building a new lab."

"What kind of test?" Lin said. "A math test?"

"Nope." I sat down on the big copper penny outside the destroyed Fruity Stars Lab. The professor said the penny had something to do with the chemical reaction required to expand things back to their normal size, but it also made a really good seat. I quickly started snapping my little pile of PIBBs together into a basic wall. Every color was represented, but the most important color for my test was the color red. Lucky for me, I had enough red blocks to fill the middle of the little test wall I was creating with a nice round target. "Not a math test. A crash test."

CHAPTER 5
A TEST FOR BRUNO

"Are you sure this is a good idea, Danny?" Lin asked.

"It's a good idea, just not sure if it's a good plan. That's why we're doing a test. We have to know if PIBBs are Microsaur-proof, and the best way to find out is to let Bruno try to tear them apart," I explained.

As soon as that lovable, puppylike, three-horned Microsaur sees as much as a pair of red gym socks, he goes absolutely nutso. It was easy to hide the tiny wall of PIBBs I'd snapped together when they were still small enough to fit inside my Shrink-A-Fied pocket, but I knew as soon as the Expand-O-Matic grew them back to their original size, Bruno would be on them in a flash.

"We better stand back," I said. No answer. I turned to look around for Lin. She was nowhere

in sight. Zip-Zap was peeking around a torn-up corner of the Fruity Stars Lab 2.0, but Lin and Bruno had disappeared.

"Lin?" I shouted as I jogged back to the Expand-O-Matic. "Where are you?"

"Go ahead and expand the PIBBs wall, Danny. I'm behind the lab, keeping Bruno calm for a minute. We're ready," she said.

Something in Lin's voice made me think there was more to her story, but the CEPs were warmed up, the wall was in place, and the only thing left to do was expand the wall.

"Okay. Here it goes," I said. The Expand-O-Matic bubbled, boiled, and burped to life. It took a little longer than the Shrink-A-Fier to get going because the Carbonic Expansion Particles inside the machine had to get up to exactly 104.3 degrees Fahrenheit. I slammed my hand down on the button. Orange Carbonic Expansion Particles shot up the coiled tube, glittered out from the showerhead nozzle, and rained down to the tiny stack of PIBBs. They grew almost immediately, and I have to admit, even I was shocked at how big they were. I always forget just how little I am when I'm Shrink-A-Fied. I had expected the little wall to be up to my stomach, not over my head.

I was trying to reach up to the top of the wall

to measure things out a little when I heard footsteps coming my way, followed by a loud "YAAAAHOOOO!"

I jumped out of the way just in time. Bruno smashed into the plastic barrier with Lin—

skateboard helmet snapped tight beneath her chin—riding on his back.

"Oh yeah! Smash it, Bruno!" Lin shouted as Bruno used his wide-crested head to batter into the wall again and again.

He stabbed at it with his nose-horn. He lifted it up with his brow tines. He smashed against it with his wide rump, and thumped his powerful tail against the wall. He pounced, and hammered, and tossed, and rammed the PIBB wall while Lin rode him like a cowgirl with a rodeo bull.

Bruno spun around like a top, winding up his powerful tail and lining it up just right. The spinning motion was too much for Lin, and I watched as Lin was sent flying through the air. She landed on the copper penny below the Expand-O-Matic's spray nozzle, laughing so hard she couldn't stand up.

Bruno's tail made direct contact with the wall, and he sent it sailing through the air, right into the smashed-up Fruity Stars Lab 2.0. It clanged off the CEP holding tank. The long, spirally coils that delivered CEPs to the nozzle were wrapped around the PIBB wall as it came to a stop.

I looked at Bruno, and he looked back at me. He had an I'm-gonna-smash-that-wall-even-more look in his eyes that I will never forget. I'll never forget it because it matched the Oh-no-what-have-I-done-don't-smash-that-wall-anymore feeling in my gut.

"No, Bruno! Stop!" I shouted, but it was too late. Bruno charged after the wall. He tore it from the coils, shoving the PIBB wall through what was left of the lab. The control unit toppled to the ground, and Bruno stepped on the big red button, sending one last shot of CEPs up through the nozzle and out on Lin's head.

As she expanded around us, Bruno dragged half of the Expand-O-Matic with him into the

woods, leaving the
other half behind, torn
to pieces and shooting out steam.

Lin thought quickly. Before Bruno could do
even more damage, she reached down and
snatched up the PIBB wall. As soon as the red
bricks were out of his view, Bruno collapsed
down on his stomach and panted over and over.

I heard a beep from inside my ear. Lin and I always wore our SpyZoom Invisible Communicators, tiny earbuds that we could hide in our ears that allowed us to communicate when we were apart. It even worked, as we'd discovered on more than one occasion, when one of us was regular-sized and one of us was super tiny.

"Can you hear me, Danny?" Lin whispered.

"Uh-huh" was all I could manage to say. The destruction all around me was too much to take

in. The lab was a total loss, and now the Expand-O-Matic was torn in two.

"Well, that was impressive," Lin said.

"Uh-huh," I said again.

"I just rode a charging, furious triceratops, and I didn't even get a scratch on me. That was impressive," Lin said.

I nodded, because I had to agree. Although at my size I was sure Lin couldn't see it. I think I was in shock.

"Oh, and I'm not the only one. The wall didn't get a scratch, either. Awesome, Danny. The test was a success," Lin said in my ear.

I blinked. I rubbed my eyes. I swallowed a dry lump in my throat.

"Danny? Are you okay?" Lin said.

From the forest behind me, I heard Pizza and Cornelia growling again. I turned and looked just as the pack of tiny-raptors came running from the trees . . . again.

CHAPTER 6
THE MASTER OF DISASTER

The pack of raptors flapped their tiny wings and squawked around me. They were trying to climb on me and get behind me. I guess they were looking for me to protect them from Pizza and Cornelia, but what could I do? I was as helpless as they were. I snapped out of my fog and started thinking. I tapped my Invisible Communicator so Lin could hear me.

"Lin. You've got to catch the twins. They are going to destroy the entire Microterium," I said.

"No problem," Lin said. "And then we can go to the zoo."

I called to Bruno for some help shooing away the oviraptors. He galloped over toward me, but stopped dead in his tracks when the twin tiny-saurus rexes growled in the trees again.

"Wait. Did you say the zoo?" I asked Lin.

"Yeah. Just because we had a little accident doesn't mean we are skipping the zoo," Lin said.

"That is *exactly* what that means. EXACTLY. Lin, this place is totally destroyed, and it's getting worse. I ruin everything. I'm the master of disaster," I said. I was covered in oviraptors, a situation I never expected to find myself in.

The twins roared out of the forest, their shiny teeth gleaming in the sunshine. They didn't look mean to me, they looked like they wanted to play. But Bruno and the oviraptors saw things differently. The oviraptors tensed up, digging their claws painfully into my arms, my shoulders, even to the top of my head. It was all too much!

"Get off me!" I shouted as I jumped and waved my arms around. Feathers floated to the ground around me as the oviraptors flapped away, looking for a safe spot that wouldn't yell at them.

"Don't worry. I got this," Lin said. Then her massive hand reached down from the sky and she picked up

Cornelia by her tail. I watched as Lin lifted her in the air and placed her inside the tin mint case that had been their temporary home since they had hatched. Pizza started running around, snapping and growling now that he had been separated from his sister.

"Come here, little guy," Lin said in what she thought was a soothing voice but to me it was as loud as thunder. Pizza tried to run away and hide from Lin's loud voice, but she scooped him up and put him in the mint tin with his sister.

"There. Problem solved," Lin said. She placed the mint tin down next to me. It was odd to see it from my tiny point of view, because it really was big enough to make a comfy home for Pizza and Cornelia. That is, until they grew up.

"Well, that's one problem down. We only have about fifty thousand more," I said as I looked around at the chaos. I started winding up the long coil hose that used to connect the Expand-O-Matic tank and spray nozzle together. "We have to get this lab out of here and start cleaning this place up."

Lin, in her large size, made quick work of the cleanup. The Fruity Stars box rose in the sky, and she tossed it out of the Microterium and into the barn-lab. "Problem number two solved. Only forty-nine thousand, nine hundred ninety-eight to go," Lin said. I looked up and saw she was wearing a gigantic smile.

"It's not funny, Lin," I explained. "Maybe you don't realize this, but if I don't fix the Expand-O-Matic I could be stuck small forever. And even worse than that, Professor Penrod will be so mad that he'll never trust us with the Microterium again."

"It's okay to chill a little, Danny. We have a few hours before he's back, right?" Lin said.

I checked the app on my phone. "Three hours and thirty-six minutes, give or take a few seconds."

"No problem. Look. Come to the zoo with me. I want to show Annie and Sam my Microbites final recipe. And the class is only one hour. We can run to your house and grab some PIBBs, build a quick lab, and be back here with more than an hour to spare," Lin said.

"How about you go to the zoo, and I'll clean the place up," I suggested. I was trying to stand Professor Penrod's bookcase back up.

Lin tipped it upright with a single fingernail. "How about we both go to the zoo, then we both come back here and clean up together. You know we're best that way. I've heard you say it before."

Beneath the bookcase, the books were all stacked in a pile. I dug through them until I found Professor Penrod's leather-bound journal. I knew inside I would find drawings of the Expand-O-Matic and plans for how to put it back together. I thumbed through the pages, then thought about it for a while. I had a lot of studying to do before I could reassemble the broken Expand-O-Matic, but it didn't do any good to put it back together unless I had somewhere to put it. I couldn't leave it out in the open, and we knew now more than ever that cardboard wasn't the answer. We needed to build a new lab out of PIBBs. And the more I thought about it, we needed to build a playpen for Pizza and Cornelia. At least until we could train them to stop chasing the pack of oviraptors.

I looked around. The place was a mess, but with Lin helping me while big, and my hands doing the details while small, things really would go faster. I tucked Professor Penrod's notebook in my backpack and looked up at Lin.

"All right. But there's no time to mess around at the zoo. It's in. Show your treats to the instructors. And get out. We have too much to do to stop by and visit the other animals. Not today," I said.

"I totally understand," Lin said. She pried open the lid to the tiny-saurus rexes' mint tin. "Climb in, Danny. There's plenty of room."

"I'm not riding in there. It's not safe," I said.

"Let me put it this way. If you ride with the twins, you know exactly what's inside that box. If you ride in the bottom of my pocket, you have no idea what you could run into," Lin said.

I sighed then let out a big breath. "All right. You have a point. Help me climb in," I said. Then I climbed on Lin's hand, and she slipped me into the mint tin with Pizza and Cornelia.

CHAPTER 7
JUST A LITTLE DETOUR

On our way out of the Microterium, Lin stuffed a few snacks in the mint tin with me and the twins. A couple of shredded pepperoni slices and a few chunks of corn dogs, complete with mustard. I wasn't too thrilled about it because it made the little mint tin smell pretty strong, but it did seem to calm down Pizza and Cornelia, so I guess it was for the best.

The mint case didn't quite fit all the way inside Lin's pocket, so I climbed to the top to try to get a look around. If I stretched on my tiptoes while balancing on Pizza's head, I could see a small view of the world as I peeked out of an airhole punched in the mint case. Which Cornelia found hilarious, by the way. Not the looking out part, the standing on her brother's head part.

"I don't know about this. Maybe we should skip the zoo," I said into the Invisible Communicator. "I've ruined everything."

"No you haven't," Lin disagreed. "It's just a little mess. We can get it all cleaned up."

"A little mess? The Expand-O-Matic is completely destroyed. Bruno smashed the Express Modulation Unit! It looks more like a Pancake Modulation Unit."

"Wait. The Expand-O-Matic makes pancakes?" Lin asked. She put her skateboard down on the sidewalk and stepped on board.

"No, no, that's not what I mean. I was making a joke. What I mean is that there is no way we should be . . ." I started, then Lin kicked off on her skateboard and the world became a blur.

I felt like I was on a rocket ship to the zoo, not on a skateboard. Lin hit a bump, then did some kind of kick-flip, and it bounced me and the twins around inside the mint case. I fell from

Pizza's head and ended up on the bottom of a pile of Microsaurs, snack scraps, and an old cotton ball that was covered in mustard and T. rex slobber.

"No more tricks!" I shouted.

"Oh, sorry, Danny. It's a habit," Lin said. The constant whirl of Lin's skateboard wheels and the wind as it rushed by was loud in my ears.

"And you two are in trouble with me, too," I said as I looked up at Pizza, who was smashed between me and Cornelia. "You've got to stop chasing everything in the Microterium that runs, because one, you're making a huge mess, and two, EVERYTHING RUNS!"

Pizza tilted his head to make eye contact. He grinned at me, then growled a gurgle sound in the back of his throat.

"I'm not kidding," I said as I peeled an oily strip of pepperoni off my shirt. I tossed it to Pizza, and he snapped it up in one bite. "It's important. Very important. I mean, Professor Penrod left us in charge of the place. Sure, we're rebuilding the Fruity Stars Lab, but it's not finished. And you two, well, let's just say that hasn't been a successful experiment. No offense," I said to Cornelia.

Cornelia smiled, then burped, then smiled even wider.

"Who are you talking to, Danny?" Lin said in my Invisible Communicator.

"Myself, I guess," I said.

I pulled my phone from my pocket just as Lin did another trick thingy. The three of us bounced up and shuffled among the snacks and cotton ball again. I nearly dropped my phone. I turned it on to check the time.

"The professor will be home in three hours and four minutes. Just thought you'd like a time check," I said to Lin.

"That's plenty of time, and good news. We're already here," Lin said. The noise of Lin's wheels stopped, and we bounced around in the mint tin one more time as she jumped off her skateboard.

Pizza growled, and Cornelia made a little noise that sounded like a giggle. Then they both growled at each other, then they both looked at me and giggled.

"It's not funny, you two. It's serious," I said.

Pizza agreed and frowned, but Cornelia went into another laughing fit. There was something seriously wrong with that laughing Microsaur. Something very wrong indeed.

"I guess that's what I get for trying to reason with a T. rex," I said. I settled down on the cotton fluff and tried to take a few deep breaths to calm down. It's a technique my dad taught me, and it helps. Well, it helps a little.

"Are you talking to yourself again, Danny?" Lin asked as she entered the zoo. I could hear people chattering all around her, but still I couldn't see a thing from inside the mint tin.

"Probably," I said.

"I do that, too, sometimes. I'm at the front gate," Lin said. "Do you have your zoo pass?"

"Um, yes, but I don't think they'll be able to read it without a microscope," I said.

"Yeah. Good point. Are you ready?" Lin asked.

"For what?" I asked. "To be stuck half the size of a grain of rice for the rest of my life? Because no, I'm not ready for that."

"No, Mr. Grumpy Pants. For class to start," Lin said, although I already knew what she was talking about.

"When you're ant-sized, it doesn't matter if you're ready for class to begin. It does, however, matter that we get back to the Microterium soon so I can, oh, I don't know, FIX THE EXPAND-O-MATIC BEFORE PROFESSOR PENROD GETS HOME," I said.

"In through the nose, out through the mouth, Danny. Breathe. Relax. Read a book. There's plenty of time. Besides, Penny isn't back from China for like three hours or something," Lin said.

"Two hours and fifty-four minutes," I said.

"In through the nose, out through the mouth, Danny. We have plenty of time. In through the nose, out through the mouth," Lin said. "Besides. I've seen you fix loads of things before. You'll get it together in no time at all."

"Sure. I can build a Slide-A-Riffic, and even then I forgot the brakes, but I have no idea where to start rebuilding one of the most important inventions of our time," I said.

89

"The most important?" Lin asked, referring to the Expand-O-Matic.

"When you are one quarter the size of a pencil eraser, the Expand-O-Matic is very important."

"That's a good point, but I believe in you. Okay. Class is starting. I'm going to find a seat. Can you see?"

I worked my way to the top of the mint case again and looked out of the airholes. "Kind of. Maybe when you sit down you could put the mint case on top of the table or something. It is jiggling a lot in here. I'm starting to get motion sickness."

Peering through the airhole, I watched as Lin followed a bunch of kids our age into the zoo's very own classroom. We'd been there before, but at my current size it looked gigantic. Junior Zookeeper classmates chatted all around us, and the twins were getting very excited. Lin walked in, found a seat at an empty desk, then pulled the mint case out of her pocket.

We rolled around inside until she placed the mint case on the desk.

"Oh no. This can't be happening," Lin said.

"What, what's going on?" I said.

"This is the biggest disaster of all time. Ever. Worse than the Expand-O-Matic getting smashed," Lin said.

"What could be worse than that?" I asked as I tried to peek through the airhole to see what Lin was talking about.

She rotated the mint case so I could get a look at the desk right next to hers.

"This," Lin whispered. "She is worse than the destroyed Expand-O-Matic."

"That's not even close to worse, but I'm confused. Why is Vicky Van-Varbles here?" I asked.

"I have no idea," Lin whispered. "Should I ask her?"

"Sure. That'd be nice," I said.

"I'm not interested in being nice, but I am curious," Lin said.

Just then, I heard a muffled voice. "Are you talking to yourself?" Vicky said.

"Yes. I mean no. I mean, not really. What I mean to say is, why are you here?" Lin said. "You weren't here for the first two classes."

"Oh, I didn't need those two classes. I probably know more about protecting endangered species and providing safe habitats than anyone in this entire classroom. Maybe even in the entire zoo. I've been to Africa, South America, and next summer we're going to feed pandas in China. I'm pretty much a world-traveling animal expert. I could practically teach the class, if they needed me to," Vicky said without taking a single breath.

"Oh boy, can you get a load of her?" Lin said to me, but Vicky obviously thought it was directed to her.

"In through your nose, out through your mouth, Lin," I said.

"A load of what? Also, I had horseback riding camp two weeks ago and Singing Stars camp last week. As you probably know, I'm a very busy girl," Vicky said. I could only see her mouth and hands through the airhole, but I could tell by the way she moved them that she was very impressed with herself.

"Last week I rode a dinosaur through a swamp, and two weeks ago I jumped from a bottle cap suspended beneath a flying lizard-bat to rescue a shiny battery so my friend and I could grow thirty-five times our size," Lin said.

"Eighty-five times our size, but who's counting," I said, which made Lin giggle.

"You're weird. I stopped playing imagination games when I was six. You should really grow up," Vicky said.

"Oh, I'll grow up all right," Lin said, which I didn't totally understand, but then she started to stand up. I heard her pop her knuckles, and I really wished I was her size so I could calm her down. I had to try my best while tiny-sized.

"Um, Lin. Can you hear this?" I asked. I took the Invisible Communicator out of my ear and held it to Pizza's stomach. It growled and gurgled. "I need your help. These guys are getting hungry and restless."

"Sure. I've got more snacks in my pocket. Just a second," Lin said as she sat back down.

"What? You brought your lunch? This is about feeding animals, not humans," Vicky said. I could almost hear the big grin on her face. "Oh, it's just mints. I don't know why you are making such a big deal about mints. I have the exact same kind of mints in my purse, and you don't see me bragging about them."

Lin huddled around the tin box, hiding it away from Vicky and the rest of the class. The lid popped open, and I had to hold back Pizza and Cornelia from jumping out.

"Hey, little critters. How are you? Want a snack?" Lin stuffed more shredded pepperoni and mustard-covered corn-dog pieces into the case with me and the twins.

"How's that?" Lin whispered to me.

"Thanks. Crisis averted," I said. "For now."

"Good. Holler if you need something," Lin said.

I could see the desk next to Lin's now. Vicky was sitting there in her purple glitter jacket. She pulled a tin of mints out of her bag and put it on the desk, then she opened the box and started talking to the mints, totally making fun of Lin.

"All right, mints. Stay minty. I'll eat you later. Is that okay with you, talking mints?" Vicky said, then she laughed at her own joke so hard I thought she was going to fall out of her chair. A couple of the kids sitting around her laughed, too, but Lin didn't think it was funny. Not one bit.

"One of these days I'm going to introduce her to what is inside my mint tin. We'll see who's laughing when she is staring up at a couple hundred T. rex teeth," Lin said.

"In through your nose, out through your mouth, Lin," I said.

Lin took a deep breath, then the class started to mumble as the instructors entered the room.

"Hello, class. I'm Annie," the taller of the two said.

"And I'm Samantha, but you can call me Sam," the other said. "And we need two volunteers."

Lin shot her hand up so fast she nearly knocked me and the twins to the floor, and I had a sneaking suspicion that Vicky's went up even faster.

CHAPTER 8
JUNIOR ZOOKEEPER'S CLASS

With the mint tin lying on top of the desk, I had a pretty good view of the class. I could see the zookeepers, Sam and Annie, and their two apes, as well as a good portion of the class. Even Vicky and her sparkly outfit.

"Okay. How about you in the bike helmet," Annie said, pointing to Lin.

"YES!" Lin said. She pumped her fist, then raced to the front of the class, leaving me and the twins behind on her desk.

"And the sparkly girl with the glasses," Sam said.

"NO!" Lin said. The instructors looked at Lin, and Lin immediately backtracked, smiling and waving her hands. "I'm only kidding. I'm such a kidder. Look at me kid."

"I like to kid, too," Annie said as she welcomed Vicky up, directing them to stand next to each other, between the apes. "Well, let us introduce you to the stars of today's first feeding experiment. This is Ella. She's a six-month-old orangutan, and she loves to climb just about anything."

"And this is Buttons. He's an eight-month-old chimpanzee, and he loves to throw things, make funny faces, and, unfortunately, stick things up his nose," Sam said, and the class exploded with laughter. The fuzzy little primates were adorable.

"We brought them here to help demonstrate something very important. It's not only good to know what to feed animals, but it's also good to know when they are full," Annie said.

Sam took over. "True. Most animals aren't all that great at knowing when to stop eating, and if we give them too much at the zoo, they will just keep on eating. Even if it makes them sick. So it's important to look for clues that the animals give that will tell us if they are hungry or full. Can you think of what those might be?"

A large boy in the back of class raised his hand. "When I'm totally full I get sleepy," he said when Annie called on him.

"Excellent. Who else?" Annie said.

"When I'm done eating I rub my belly," said another kid.

"Yeah, apes and monkeys do that as well. They are a lot like us," Sam said. "How about you?" She pointed to someone behind me that I couldn't see from inside the mint tin.

"When I'm done eating sometimes I burp." The class laughed again.

"That's a good one," Annie said. "Those are all great signs, and I hope our volunteers are paying attention."

"Okay, you two, the class has given you some good ideas. Now it's time to put them to the test. I have one banana here, but two apes. Which would normally be a big problem, but one of these little guys has already had its lunch. You two get to look for clues and decide which one gets the banana," Sam explained.

From where I was it looked like the orangutan was almost asleep. She slumped in Annie's arms like she was being held by a comfy, jungle canopy cradle. She took a handful of Annie's hair and twisted it slowly with her fingers. Then she did the cutest thing of all—she started sucking her thumb.

The whole class let out a group "Awwwwww" as we started hearing the sucking noise.

In contrast, the chimp was wiggling in Sam's arms. He was trying to steal her hat and put it on his head. Or perhaps eat it. I couldn't tell.

I looked up at Lin through the hole and saw her rubbing her chin like I do when I'm thinking real hard. I could tell she was about to point to the chimp, a decision I agreed with, when Vicky jumped forward and spoke first.

"It's Buttons. I know it. Look at him. He's so hungry he's almost crying," Vicky said.

Buttons stuck out his tongue, then grinned real wide, showing the class his big white teeth. Everyone laughed at the adorable chimp.

"Doesn't look like he's crying to me," Lin said. "But he is rubbing his tummy. He's full. Totally full."

"Are you sure?" Sam said as she held the wiggly chimp in her arms. I thought Vicky was right. He was the hungry one. But just then Lin's eyes narrowed.

"Actually, Sparkles here is wrong. It's Ella," Lin said. "She looks hungry."

"Look. Ella is practically falling asleep in Annie's arms," Vicky said as the orange ape closed her eyes for a second, then opened them again and smiled up at Annie lovingly. "It's Buttons," Vicky said. "Isn't that right, Buttons?" Vicky asked the chimpanzee directly, which I had to admit was a pretty good idea.

Buttons shook his head then blew out a BRRRAPT! through his big lips.

"Told ya. He's full," Lin said. "I've decided. It's Ella. She's the hungry one."

"Are you sure?" Annie asked.

"Yep," Lin said. "She's starving."

"All right. Suit yourself, but I'm not feeding that orange monkey," Vicky said.

Lin picked up the banana and started peeling it. "I'll be glad to. And besides, she's an ape, not a monkey. Isn't that right, Ella?"

Ella screeched and pointed into her open mouth.

"Are you sure you're sure?" Sam said. "Sometimes animals play tricks on us."

"I think they're trying to give you a hint, Lin," I said from inside the mint tin. I didn't have the best view of the experiment, but there was something that didn't quite seem right to me.

"Am I missing something?" Lin asked me quietly in the Invisible Communicator.

"What did you say?" Annie asked.

"Oh, don't worry about her. Lin's been talking to herself all day," Vicky said. "Go ahead, Lin. Feed the orange monkey." The class started chanting, *Ella, Ella, Ella,* as Lin finished peeling the banana.

"She's not a monkey, Vicky! Ella is an ape. A hungry little ape," Lin said, and she stepped forward and handed the banana to Ella.

At first, I thought everything was going to be fine. Ella sat up in Annie's arms as she inspected the banana. She sniffed it. She licked it. Then she turned to Lin, stuck out her hand, and smashed half of the banana all over Lin's favorite shirt.

Once again, the class exploded with laughter. Only this time, there were some groans and moans mixed in. Vicky was laughing so hard I thought she was going to fall over, but Lin wasn't giving up that easy. She scraped the banana off her shirt and held it in her hands.

"It's okay, Ella. I understand," Lin said. She held out a mountain of whitish, yellowish mush to Ella. The little ape looked at Lin and smiled so wide you could count all her teeth. "Go ahead. It's all mashed up and ready."

The bright orange ape reached out and took the handful of mashed bananas and stuffed them in her mouth. The class went silent for a few seconds, then they cheered.

"Very, VERY good, Lin. That was incredible. You have the makings of a true zookeeper," Annie said. "How did you know to keep trying to feed Ella?"

"Well, I like to play with my food, too," Lin said.

"Brilliant," Sam said.

I peered over at Vicky, and she wasn't laughing anymore. Her eyebrows tilted down toward the center of her face, and her right nostril flared as her mouth turned down in a frown.

"That really was brilliant, Lin. I'm super impressed," I said.

"Thanks, Danny," Lin said.

"Who's Danny?" Sam asked.

"Oh, no, I said Annie. Thanks, ANNIE," Lin covered quickly.

"All right, class. Who wants to go feed the otters?" Annie asked.

"Will they smash oysters on our shirts?" someone in the back of the class asked, and everyone laughed again.

"Only if you're lucky," Annie said. Two new

helpers came in the room and took Ella and
Buttons.

"Say good-bye to Ella and Buttons," Sam said.

The class waved good-bye to the apes, then
they followed Annie out of the classroom. Vicky
and Lin were the last two out, and Sam came up
to them holding a bright yellow shirt.

"Sorry about the banana mash. I hope this
will make up for it." Sam handed the shirt to Lin.

Now, getting a free shirt from the zoo is cool. But everyone knows that getting a free official *Zoo Helper* T-shirt from an actual zookeeper is even cooler!

"Jeez. Thanks. You didn't need to do that. I'm really fine with a little smashed banana on my shirt," Lin said, which I knew was absolutely the truth.

"It's no problem," Sam said.

"Do all the volunteers get a shirt?" Vicky asked.

"No, sorry. Not this time. We save these for volunteers who are covered in smashed bananas. Thanks for your help, though," Sam said. "Run along and catch up with the class while your friend here changes. There's a private room back there." Sam pointed to a room in the back.

"Fine. I'm sure the otters need my help anyway," Vicky said.

"That's the spirit," Sam said. "See you soon."

"Um, hey, Sam," Lin said as she dug in her pockets and pulled out a little plastic bag of Microbites. "I was wondering what you thought about these snacks."

From my point of view, I could only see half of Sam, but she took the bag from Lin, unzipped it, and gave the treats a sniff. "Interesting," she said. She pulled one out and inspected it closer. "What are they for?"

"Well, I was thinking they might be good for small birds, parrots maybe. I don't know, maybe even reptiles," Lin said. I was pretty impressed that she was giving such good hints, while still keeping the Microsaurs a secret.

"Well, I'm not sure about the raisins. They have a lot of sugar in them. Maybe something more like sunflower seeds, which are packed with protein. But the oats are a great idea." Sam sniffed them again. "Is that peanut butter?"

I could see Lin grinning proudly through the cracked-open lid of my box. "Yup. One-hundred-percent-natural, no-preservatives-added peanut butter. It's one of my favorite snacks, so I thought they might like it, too," Lin said.

"Well, you were right. I think these are a great healthy snack for birds, parrots, and small

reptiles. Maybe for zookeepers, too," Sam said, then she popped one in her mouth. Lin laughed, and Sam joined her. "Okay, keep the raisins."

"Or maybe half raisins and half sunflower seeds," Lin said as she took the bag back from Sam.

"Perfect!" Sam agreed.

"Thanks," Lin said. "I'm going to change now. I smell like a monkey's birthday party," Lin said.

Then she took her new shirt and ran to the changing room. On her way, she carefully pressed the lid of the mint tin closed again, securing us in place. Her hands were obviously still slathered in bananas, because she smeared the top of the case and even stuffed a little in through the airholes. Pizza and Cornelia surprised me by licking up the banana mash like it was their favorite snack.

"Well, guys, that was exciting," I said to Pizza and Cornelia, who growled quietly as I scratched their noses, trying to keep them as calm as possible. "Now let's talk Lin out of the otter tank. I think we've seen enough adventure for one day."

But before I could settle in and relax among the cotton balls, food scraps, and the twin tiny-saurus rexes, I heard Vicky's voice as she came bursting back in the classroom.

"Sorry. I forgot my mints," Vicky said.

"Oh, here they are," Sam said. My world

bounced and shook as the zookeeper mistakenly picked up the wrong box of mints and handed them to Vicky.

"Thanks. See you at the otters," Vicky said as she dropped us in the bottom of her purse. Or at least that's what I thought it was because it smelled like bubble gum and perfume, and a couple flecks of glitter fell into the tin through the airholes.

"I was wrong. Looks like our adventures are still under way," I said. Pizza and Cornelia roared in agreement, and all I could do was hope that the zoo was noisy enough to cover the sound of their voices.

I jiggled around inside my little tin box. One moment, I was on top of the twins, then after a few bouncy steps, I found myself on the bottom of the pile again. Pepperoni and corn-dog chunks flew through the air. Dino tails slapped the sides

of the case, and I had to swoosh out of the way
to keep from being accidentally caught in Pizza's
open and not-so-happy mouth.

The whole time, Cornelia laughed like she
was at a clown birthday party at the premiere of
the funniest movie ever made while eating a

bucket of Sugar Squidgees covered in extra sugar. Like I said, there's something wrong with that girl.

I tapped the Invisible Communicator in my ear, turning it on to talk to my best friend. "Lin, I think we have a problem. A very big problem."

CHAPTER 9
WE'RE DOWN HERE!

"Is this about the Expand-O-Matic again?" Lin asked.

"Worse. Much worse. We've been kidnapped," I said in the most calm voice a kidnapped, Shrink-A-Fied guy with two endangered tiny-saurus rex twins could be.

"What?" Lin shouted, and the Invisible
Communicator nearly popped out of my ear.

"Too loud, TOO LOUD!" I said.

"But wait. I just changed my shirt, and I see
the mint tin right there on the desk," Lin said.

"That's Vicky's mint tin. She has yours. I mean, she has US!" I said.

"I knew she was up to something," Lin said.

"Okay, no. It wasn't really her fault. It was totally an accident, but that's not the point. We are still tumbling around in the bottom of a very glittery bag," I explained.

"I'm on my way! The class was heading to the otters. Do you hear anything otterish?" Lin said.

"I think I can hear squawking. A lot of squawking," I said. The twins could hear it, too, and they made a noise that sounded like a growl-squawk in return.

"Could you be by the parrots? I'm almost there, but I don't see Vicky," Lin said.

"We just passed the seals. I can hear them barking and it smells like fish," I explained.

"That's definitely on the way to the otter house. Hang on. I'll be right there," Lin said.

Images of her darting through the crowd

popped into my mind. As she ran, Lin kept
saying "sorry" and "excuse me" and "watch out!"

Sounds and smells drifted by me as we
traveled through the zoo. The twins were getting
restless again, digging through the food scraps

in the case, and really making the place a mess. I smelled cotton candy and hot dogs, and I knew we'd passed the Snack Shack. The smell of peanuts and hay and the trumpety cry of an elephant meant we were getting close. The otters live right across from the elephant environment.

"I'm here," Lin said in my ear. She was breathing heavy, out of breath.

"I think we're close. I can hear splashing water, and it smells kind of fishy," I said.

"The whole class is here, but I don't see Vicky. What else can you see?" Lin asked.

"Nothing. Purple light. Smells like perfume and fish. That's all I can offer," I said. "I'm starting to freak out a little, Lin."

"Me too. I can't see Vicky anywhere," she said. "And the class is already feeding the otters. Vicky wouldn't miss that, would she?"

The swaying and bouncing motion stopped, and I knew Vicky had arrived at the destination for the next step of her plans. Those plans, I had a feeling, included opening the mint tin case and discovering two tiny dinosaurs and one tiny me. I was nearly frozen with fear as I listened carefully for clues, but I couldn't hear anything that would help. Perfume, pizza, and corn-dog smells filled my nose as I took a deep breath in, but nothing else came to help me discover where we were.

"Danny, I can't see her anywhere. I need a clue," Lin said.

I looked around inside the dark mint tin box. We were trapped, and I knew that if I didn't act fast it would be a disaster. *Another* disaster. I'd already destroyed the Fruity Stars Lab, put two precious Microsaurs in danger, and busted the Expand-O-Matic today. I wasn't about to let Vicky discover us, too. I leaned my shoulder against the top of the box and pushed, but the lid wouldn't budge.

"Guys. I need your help," I said to the twins. "We've got to get out of here, and I mean NOW!"

The twins didn't really know what was going on, but they were excited by my actions. Pizza joined in first, shoving his wide head against the lid of the box. But no luck. It wouldn't move a smidge.

"I think I see Vicky," Lin said. "She's right in the front of the class. Right against the glass otter tank window. Hang on, Danny, I'm coming!"

"Come on, Corney. Help us out, would ya?" I said as Pizza and I strained against the tin lid with all our might. It creaked, then moaned, but it didn't budge. It felt like the banana muck mixed with Vicky's purse glitter had basically glued the mint tin shut.

"Stop! Thief!" Lin shouted in my ear. "You stole my mint tin!"

I could hear Vicky's voice among the crowd noise, and she sounded genuinely surprised.

"Who me? A thief? What are you talking about, Lin?" Vicky said.

"You stole my mint tin, and I need it back. NOW!" Lin said.

"I did NOT steal anything from you. You've lost your marbles," Vicky said.

"No, I've lost my mint tin, and it's in your bag. See, this one right here. It's yours," Lin said. I couldn't see her, but I imagined her holding out Vicky's mint tin that she'd left behind in class.

"No. This is my mint tin right here," Vicky said. We began to rise in the purplish dark of the purse as Vicky lifted us out. "Ooh. Gross," Vicky said. "This is absolutely disgusting. It is covered in banana goo. You're right. This is definitely yours, not mine."

"STOP! That is MY TINY-SAURUS REX!" Lin shouted, and the crowd around us stopped talking at once. The only sound I could hear was the otters swimming in their tank.

The sunshine beamed down on me as Vicky opened the lid of our mint tin. I was doing my best to convince the twins to hide beneath the snack scraps and the cotton ball. We were all covered in a thick layer of mustard camouflage, but still I was totally freaking out that we'd just been caught!

"Oh my gosh! It's even worse on the inside! I'm going to hurl! These aren't mints at all," Vicky said. Then she made a gagging noise that made *me* want to gag.

"Step away from the mint tin and nobody is going to be fed to the lions today," Lin said.

Vicky kept making the gagging noises. But she dropped the mint case on the window ledge of the otter cage. "You can keep my mint tin. I don't want it anymore. You are the worst, Lin. The WORST!" was the last thing I heard her say as she disappeared into the crowd.

We were totally exposed for a second, hiding inside the open box. But then, in a flash, Lin was there to rescue us. She scooped up the mint tin and turned to face the gawking crowd.

"Well, that's it, folks. That's the end of our new one-act play, *The Troubled Waters of the Otter House*. Go ahead and move along to the next

exhibit, and we'll be doing the show again soon,"
Lin said, waving her hands at the crowd to shoo
them away.

Through the airhole I could see the crowd
shaking their heads in confusion, but after a
couple of seconds of Lin's shooing, they went

right back to their busy lives. Lin waited for them to leave, then she opened the case and stared in at us with wide eyes. "Are you guys in there? Are you okay?" she said.

I waved up at her. My arms were covered in yellow mustard.

"We're down here," I said. "A little roughed up, but we're fine."

Lin opened Vicky's old mint tin case and dumped her mints in the trash as we walked toward the zoo exit. Then she put me and the twins in the new, mustard-and-snack-free tin. It smelled minty fresh, and Cornelia started licking the walls immediately.

"What do you say we get out of here?" Lin asked.

"I say that is the best idea you've had all day."

CHAPTER 10
PIBBS TO THE RESCUE

B efore returning to the Microterium, Lin whizzed by my house to pick up the big box of PIBBs I kept in my bedroom closet. The trip there had gone as smooth as it could, but still, it took time to travel from the zoo, to my house, and then back to Professor Penrod's house.

By the time we left my house, the smell of tiny-saurus rex pepperoni-and-corn-dog burps mixed with the overpowering smell of mints was making me dizzy, so I rode in Lin's shirt pocket for the last leg of our journey.

I tapped on my Invisible Communicator to call Lin. "Hey, Lin. I almost forgot to ask. Did I hear you shout tiny-saurus rex to that zoo crowd?"

"Uh, maybe. Okay, yes," Lin said as she leaned and screeched around the corner. "But I needed a distraction. Icky Vicky had your very life in her hands!"

"I understand, but maybe yell something like 'FREE DOUGHNUTS' next time. We're already living on the edge by taking the twins out of the Microterium. We don't want people asking questions about Microsaurs," I said. Lin crouched down to zoom under a low-hanging tree branch that covered the sidewalk, then shot back up, kick-flipped her skateboard, then tucked as we headed downhill, gaining more speed every second.

"Sorry," Lin said. "I panicked."

Which I could also understand. "Talk about panic. Professor Penrod will be home in one hour and thirteen minutes, and we need to build a new Fruity Stars Lab 3.0, make a special place for the twins, and fix the Expand-O-Matic. That's not one hour's worth of work, that's more like days of work."

"We'll be fine," Lin said, sounding totally calm as we rocketed down the sidewalk like a fireball on a skateboard. "We can work together."

"Speaking of that. While riding around in a mint tin all day, I've come up with some plans," I said.

"I was hoping you'd say that," Lin said as she jumped from her skateboard. We were back at Penrod's house, and she slipped through the iron bars to enter his backyard.

"Well, if you want to build a quick, safe lab for us out of PIBBs while you're big, I can get started on the Expand-O-Matic repairs. I've been studying the plans in the professor's notebook, and I think I can get it working again."

"I'm sure you can. But what about the lab? Do you have plans for the lab? I'm not sure what to build," Lin said. She approached the old barn door that would take us to the secret Microsaur sanctuary.

"I don't have plans, but I have ideas. It just needs to be big enough for Professor Penrod's books and lab equipment. Oh, and of course it needs to protect the Expand-O-Matic. I don't even think it needs a floor at this point. Just put it down in the dirt, and we can worry about floors later," I said.

"Okay. That sounds easy," Lin said.

"It will be. And we also need something for the twins. Like a big fence or something that we can keep them in until we have time to train them better. You can build that out of PIBBs, too," I suggested.

"Okay. I can do that," Lin said. "Any other suggestions?" Lin lowered the back wall of the barn-lab, revealing the Microterium.

"Yeah. Three. Number one, no red bricks," I said.

"Of course. Makes perfect sense," Lin said.

"Number two. Hurry. This doesn't need to be

the greatest thing ever built. These are PIBBs. We can always add on more stuff later," I said.

"Gotcha. No red bricks, and make it quick," Lin said. "Can do."

"And number three. Be creative and have fun. That's when you always come up with the best ideas," I said.

Lin stepped into the Microterium and placed me down among the mess of the destroyed Fruity Stars Lab. It wasn't as bad as I remembered, but there was still a ton of work to do. Bruno and Honk-Honk were sitting in the shade, quietly watching as the oviraptors pecked at the ground and squawked.

"All right. Let's get this going," I said.

As I dragged the scattered parts of the Expand-O-Matic back to one central spot, Lin worked on building the new Fruity Stars Lab 3.0 around me. Occasionally, I had her lift the heavy parts for me, and from time to time she asked

my advice about the lab. It was nice working together like this, and things were starting to take shape.

I could already tell that the new lab was going to work out great. Using clear bricks, Lin added skylights to the roof to brighten the place up, then she added windows in the side walls, which was great because they let in a nice breeze but still offered loads more protection than the cardboard box. Now she was working on the new playpen area for the twins, while I was ready to begin assembling the Expand-O-Matic.

I quickly got lost in my own thoughts, studying the plans for the Expand-O-Matic and trying to match parts as best I could. Time flew by, and I didn't notice that my hour and thirteen minutes had nearly evaporated until I tightened the last circular momentum bolt into place and stepped back to check out my work. The machine looked pretty good, especially with new brightly colored PIBB walls protecting it. I tapped on my Invisible Communicator.

"How's it going, Lin?" I asked.

"Look out the back window and check for yourself," Lin said. "I have a nice surprise for you."

I walked over to the back of the lab and leaned out the window. Lin had truly outdone herself. She'd dug out a nice cliff wall below the back of the new lab. Then, using the cliff wall as a starting point, Lin had built a huge play area for Pizza and Cornelia. Bright white, yellow, green, and blue bricks lined the playpen twice as high as a basketball hoop, blocking off enough space for the twins to run and play. A gate hung from shiny black hinges, and I watched Lin try it out with easy motions, although I knew it would be a lot harder to push open at my size. She'd placed a tennis ball in there for them, and Cornelia was already trying to rip all the fluff off it, while Pizza was busy sniffing the ground,

searching for worms or other nice things to eat.

"So. What do you think?" Lin asked.

"I think it's perfect! They look so happy," I said.

"They are happy, and it's big enough for them to grow. I'm pretty proud of my new creation," Lin said.

"You should be. And I think I'm ready to try the Expand-O-Matic again," I said. "Wanna come watch me grow?"

"Of course. That's my favorite part," Lin said. I was realizing that Lin had a lot of favorite parts. Pretty much everything she saw became her new favorite part.

I flicked the switch to turn on the CEP warmer, checked the temperature gauge, then walked out the door Lin had installed next to the Expand-O-Matic. I looked to make sure the copper penny was aligned perfectly beneath the carbonic dispersal nozzle and smiled as I heard the Expand-O-Matic bubble and gurgle from inside the new lab.

"I think it's going to work just fine," I said to Lin.

"I'm sure it will. Give it a try already, would ya?"

I ran back into the lab, hit the button to free a little burst of CEPs, then ran back out to the penny to wait for my orange shower.

The machine coughed. And I waited.

The machine burped and boiled. And still, I waited.

And waited. And waited. AND WAITED!

"Is everything okay?" Lin asked.

A single drop of bright orange Carbonic Expansion Particle liquid dripped from the nozzle and fell right on top of my head. It was just enough to make my hair grow longer. So long, in fact, that it reached down past my toes and flowed over the edges of the penny. I felt like screaming. All the hope I had stored up while

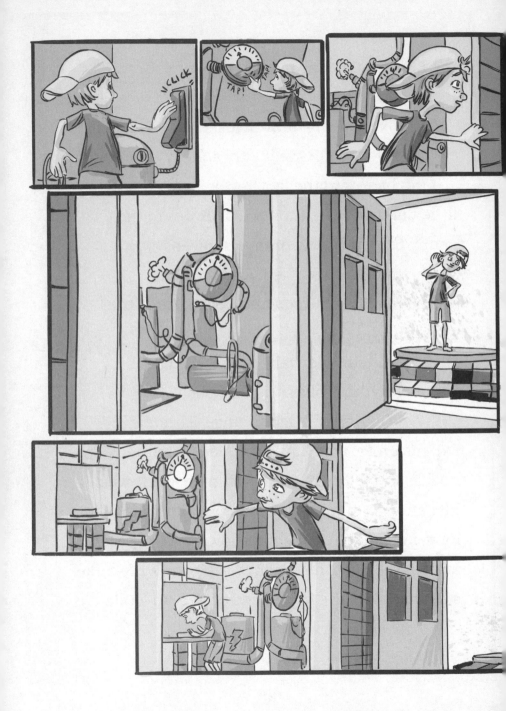

rebuilding the Expand-O-Matic melted away in an instant as I stood on the copper penny in dire need of a haircut.

Just then my phone blipped, and I saw something I did not want to see: Professor Penrod's smiling face. I didn't want to answer it, but what could I do? Ignore him and hope the problems I'd created would go away? Well, that would never happen, so I tapped on my phone, answering his call.

I pushed the hair out of my eyes, then tried to smile a little. "Hello, Professor Penrod," I said.

"Well, hello there, Danny," the professor said, and my worries only grew as I could tell from the video on my phone that he had just entered the barn-lab. The professor had returned.

"Oh my goodness! It's Penny," Lin shouted, and it felt like a thunderstorm erupted in my earpiece. She jumped up and took a few big steps, shaking the ground I stood on like an earthquake.

The image on my phone went bonkers for a minute, then it came back into focus as Lin hugged Professor Penrod so tight I thought he was going to crumple over.

"Ha-ha! It's so good to see you again, Lin. And you're just in time. I need you to identify a strange, hairy creature on my phone," the professor said. He turned the phone so Lin could see me on the other end.

"Danny? Is that you?" Lin said as the two of them smiled into the camera.

"Yeah, it's me," I said slowly. I wanted to run away and hide in the deep forest of the

Microterium forever. But I knew it was too late. The Expand-O-Matic hadn't worked. I had to face the problems I'd created, and the two people waving back to the hairy beast on the camera were the only two people on earth who could help me out. "And well, Professor Penrod, there's something I need to tell you. . . ."

"That you need a haircut? We've noticed," Lin said, and the two of them burst into laughter.

I silently reconsidered my plan to live on my own in the wilds of the Microterium. I could survive on my own. Especially if I knew where Lin kept her stash of Microbites.

CHAPTER 11

HE'S BACK!

As the laughter died down, Lin must have noticed my annoyed face because she said, "Relax, Danny. We're gonna shrink down right now so you can tell Penny in person."

"NO!" I shouted back. They both jumped, shocked at my sudden response. "You can't shrink yet. In fact, you might never be able to shrink again."

"What? Why not?" Professor Penrod asked.

"Sure we can. The Shrink-A-Fier is right here, ready to go," Lin said.

"Well, of course you *can* shrink down. It's just that you might not ever be able to expand back up," I said. Professor Penrod looked confused. Lin looked like she finally knew what I was talking about. I took a few steps toward the lab, my heavy hair dragging behind me, then I was YANKED to a stop so hard I fell back and landed right on my rump.

I looked over my shoulder to see Bruno was following close behind me. So close, in fact, that he was standing and slobbering a little on my new hairdo.

"Oh, come on!" I shouted. I stood back up, grabbed my hair in both hands, and tried to pull it out from under Bruno. "This is ridiculous!"

Bruno didn't understand my frustration. He wagged his tail, slobbered a little more, then made a chuffing-barking sound.

"Dude. You've got to get off my hair!" I said, which is definitely a sentence I never thought I'd say in my entire life. Bruno tilted his head and looked at me like I was trying to teach him algebra.

Realizing that pulling my hair from under Bruno was not going to work, I went to the big puppylike Microsaur and tried to push him off. "Move, you big lump of horns," I said as I heaved into Bruno's back. He finally got the idea, stood up, and walked toward the PIBBs lab.

I gathered my hair up in my arms and sighed. Time was up. There was no more putting off what had to be done. I had to tell Professor

Penrod the truth. All of it. Every drop, even though I was super worried that he'd be so disappointed that he'd never let me back in his Microterium ever again. I dragged my hair into the lab after Bruno, put the camera down on the dice that served as a lab table, then sat down on a pushpin Lin had helped me push into the ground earlier for a chair.

I let out a deep breath, then:

"Okay. Here it goes. Basically, I'm probably stuck little forever, except for my hair, but that's

only part of the story. I am the master of disasters. While trying to protect the egg that held the twins, I led an entire pack of wild oviraptors right to the Fruity Stars Lab. They nearly tore it to shreds," I started.

"Well, actually, it was Honk-Honk who led them to the lab," Lin said.

"True, but we were the ones that tied the egg to Honk-Honk's back, so it was really our fault, not hers," I explained. "But that's only the start of the troubles. After chasing the egg and Honk-Honk all throughout the Microterium, we ended up directly below it, once again leading the pack of tiny-raptors back to the lab. Only this time, Honk-Honk had nothing to do with it. The second time, they *really* destroyed the place."

"Why didn't you tell me? I always like to know how things are going while I'm away from the Microterium," Professor Penrod said.

"We didn't want to worry you," Lin said.

"And we thought we could fix it before you got back from China," I said.

"I appreciate that, but not knowing is sometimes worse than worrying," Professor Penrod said. "Besides, I might have been able to help."

"We thought about that as well. But in the end, we decided to take care of it ourselves. We made a new Fruity Stars Lab," I said.

"I might have broken the world record for fastest time eating a box of Fruity Stars cereal without milk. We're still going to look into that, right, Danny?" Lin said, looking into the camera.

"Um, sure. Soon as we can. Back to the story. We put the new Fruity Stars Lab 2.0 in place, and it lasted about thirty seconds before Pizza and Cornelia spooked the other Microsaurs and destroyed the new lab before we had even set up shop," I said.

"Who?" Professor Penrod asked.

"The twin tiny-saurus rexes. That's right. You haven't met them yet. They are the most amazing things EVER! Just wait until you see how cute they are when they growl and show their teeth!" Lin did her impression of a grinning T. rex, looking an awful lot like the goofy Cornelia.

"Oooh, scary! I am excited to meet them," Professor Penrod said.

"Well, turns out letting two wild tiny-saurus rexes roam the Microterium was also a mistake. They terrified the other Microsaurs, especially Zip-Zap and the oviraptors," I said. "I should have known it would be a problem."

"Well, it's true. You might have seen that one coming," Professor Penrod said.

"We both thought that they were ready to explore the Microterium on their own," Lin said. "But it didn't work out too well, did it?"

"Not one bit. We left them here unsupervised, and they scared Bruno, Zip-Zap, and the tiny-raptors enough to immediately trash the new lab! Turns out Microsaurs and cardboard labs are a recipe for disaster," I said.

"It was always meant to be a temporary solution," Professor Penrod said. The camera shifted as he moved toward the Microterium. "It looks like you've found a more permanent solution, though."

"Yes, but that's when the REAL disaster started. While stress-testing the PIBBs with Bruno, the Expand-O-Matic was destroyed. Lin was expanded just in time, but I wasn't so lucky," I said.

The professor's face went very grave. "I see. That IS a serious problem."

"I knew it," I said, feeling more guilty than ever. "I wanted to fix it before you got back, but . . ." I trailed off with a sigh, my shoulders slumping.

Lin didn't look much better. Her head was tilted down toward the ground, and she held her helmet in her hands. She looked over at me, then started to explain the rest of our day as fast as she could. "Then I took microsized Danny and the twins to the zoo. They got covered in mustard and bananas. Nearly got discovered by my nemesis, Icky Vicky Van-Varbles, too. And almost drowned in the otter tank. Okay, I might have made that last part up, but it kind of fits with the rest of our crazy day. Then we came back here and installed the new lab. The Fruity Stars Lab 3.0," Lin said all in one breath.

Professor Penrod's eyes were wide. It looked like he was at a lost for words. It was a lot of information to take in all at once.

"Once we got back, I tried to follow your drawings from your field guide to reassemble the

Expand-O-Matic. I thought that I did everything just right, but well . . . Let's just say it's more of a Long-Hair-O-Matic now," I said as I pushed a chunk of hair away from my face. "It turns on. It warms up. But something is just not quite right. I can't get it to work," I said. A dry lump formed in my throat, and I knew that any second now tears would start rolling down my cheeks.

"So, that's why you can never shrink again. Because if you do, the very best that can happen is that we'll all end up super tiny humans with superlong hair. And trust me. It's not as good as it sounds," I said.

"Honestly, it sounds horrible, Danny," Lin said.

"It does sound horrible, and it is even worse than that," I said. "A hundred times worse, at least." I sniffed back tears and glared down at my hair pooled across the floor, waiting for Penrod to scold us or to tell me that I was stuck like this forever.

"I'll be honest. You're correct. This isn't a good situation, and it would have been much better if you'd told me earlier what was going on. If nothing else, I could have provided you with advice on dealing with the newly hatched tiny-saurus rexes, which might have avoided some of the other disasters," Professor Penrod said.

I heard Lin sniff next to me. Out of the corner of my eye I saw her wipe her nose on the back of her arm. I gulped, then braved a quick look at

Professor Penrod, and I was shocked to see that he was actually smiling.

"But worrying about things in the past is better left for paleontologists," Professor Penrod said with a wink. "I think we should turn our attention to the future. What do you say we work on getting you back to normal, Danny?" the professor asked.

I hurried and wiped a tear from my eye, hoping to catch it before anyone noticed. "I think that's a good idea. Sure."

"Well, then. Let's turn that camera on the Expand-O-Matic, and you can talk me through what you did. I'm sure we'll discover the issue together, and we'll have it fixed in a jiffy," Professor Penrod said.

"And if not, we can at least shrink you a pair of scissors so you can give yourself a haircut," Lin added.

"Ha-ha. Very funny," I said.

CHAPTER 12
A PROPER DIAGNOSIS

Picking up the phone and spinning it slowly around, I gave Professor Penrod a quick view of the new lab.

"While we were building the lab—well, while Lin was building the lab, I thought it would be nice if we put the Expand-O-Matic in its own room. It's just behind this door," I said as I let

myself in. "Welcome to the Expand-O-Room."

"It's nice to see it up close and in person," Professor Penrod said. "My compliments to the architect. Making it out of PIBBs was brilliant. I never would have thought of that. So simple. So easy to add on to in the future. I love it."

"That's what we thought. I have plans to add a pool with a real diving board soon," Lin said.

"That sounds perfectly peachy, Lin," Professor Penrod said.

I waited while Lin grinned and Professor Penrod messed up her hair, then we continued.

"So, I followed your blueprints as close as I could, but I had to make some adjustments because a few pieces were either lost or destroyed in all the chaos," I said, aiming the camera at the Expand-O-Matic itself.

"Understandable," Professor Penrod said. "You're doing a fabulous job here. Can you take me around and show me the new modifications?"

"I had a little trouble hooking the condenser coil to the CBR percolation redactor," I said, pulling the leather journal out of my backpack and flipping to the page with Professor Penrod's blueprint drawing of the Expand-O-Matic. I showed it to the camera. "See. Right here."

"Oh yes. That part was a little tricky. I had to use a modified spring pin assembly. But that's not the most difficult part. You see, I had to figure out a way to attach a lint filter to the inlet valve without compromising the CEP flow, while at the same time allowing for the release of oxygen bubbles due to rapid expansion," Professor Penrod said.

I followed the camera up the Expand-O-Matic's condenser coil until I found something that looked like a steam whistle. "Is that what you used this tap adaptor for?" I asked.

"Precisely. But can you zoom in a little?" Professor Penrod asked.

I reached up as high as I could to give Professor Penrod a better view of the little steam whistle.

"Yes, that's one of the issues. Probably not our major problem, but something we should fix nonetheless. Lin, please start a list for us. Item number one, upside-down tap adaptor," Professor Penrod said.

The professor tilted up his phone, and I saw Lin scratch down notes on a piece of paper. "Upside-down helicopter. Got it," she said.

"Close enough, Lin," the professor said with a smile. "What's next? Let's carry on."

"Well, Bruno flattened the bushing bar connector, so I had to improvise." I ducked beneath the CEP tank, turning on the flashlight on my phone for a bit of extra light, and focused the camera. "Can you see it?"

"Yes. Is that an elastic compensating ring?" Professor Penrod asked.

"It sure is," I said.

"Brilliant. I used a less flexible method, but this is a nice improvement. It should increase the particle flow by ten, maybe fifteen percent!"

"I was hoping for twenty," I said, and Professor Penrod laughed so hard he had to sit down. "I learned this method from my dad. He did something like this on his Smell-O-Tronic device he invented for SpyZoom."

"Impressive. Well done, Danny," the professor said.

"What are you writing down, Lin?" I asked. It appeared like Lin was still taking notes behind

Professor Penrod as she bent over her paper, her pencil moving so fast it was blurry on my video feed. "Did you get the notes on the flexible bushing bar connector?"

"Uh, no. I thought you guys were just making up words. Sorry. I got a little distracted. Don't mind me," Lin said, then she went back to her paper and pencil. The professor and I continued our Expand-O-Matic inspection. We searched every inch of the machine before Professor Penrod's keen eye picked up the problem.

"Wait! Danny, I think I figured it out. Can you zoom back in on the unidirectional inlet valve again for me, please?" he said.

The valve looked kind of like a pair of butterfly wings, and it allowed warm CEPs to flow into the housing unit before they were shot out.

"Yep. That's our problem. For sure. The valve's broken."

I studied the valve in the phone's light and sure enough, there was a tiny crack.

"Oh, I see . . . so how do I fix it?"

"You can't."

"What do you mean it can't be fixed? Does that mean Danny's going to be tiny forever?" Lin asked, looking up from her drawings.

"Certainly not. It just needs to be replaced, and I have the spare part right here in the barn-lab . . . which, now that I think of it, is a horrible place to keep replacement parts. This is the second time that someone's been stuck with a broken Expand-O-Matic. I should really shrink all my replacement parts and move them to the new lab where I can actually get to them when I need them," Professor Penrod said.

"So, we're shrinking? Great! I've got six new haircut designs for Danny to choose from!" Lin said, bounding to her feet.

Lin showed me her drawings. She was very proud of herself, and they did make Professor Penrod laugh.

"I may not understand what parts make the Expand-O-Matic work, but I do understand haircut jokes," Lin said, which made me laugh as well.

"All right, let's shrink and rescue that tiny friend of ours, Lin," Professor Penrod said. "It's getting late, and it will take a bit to get the part over to the new lab."

"No it won't! We've got one more surprise for you, too, Penny. The Slide-A-Riffic. It was a lot more fun this morning, but Danny pooped the party by installing brakes. But don't worry. I'll control the brakes so it's still loads of fun," Lin said.

"The Slide-A-Riffic. That sounds positively delightful," Professor Penrod said.

"Oh, you have no idea. You are in for a real treat," Lin said. "See you in a jiff, Danny."

Lin clicked their side of the camera off, and I was left alone in the Microterium once again with Bruno and the Microsaurs. Only this time, it wasn't so bad. I knew that soon I'd be rescued.

I was about to sit down and relax until they arrived, and then I remembered something terrifying. I hadn't shown Lin how to use the new, untested, and probably unreliable brakes.

CHAPTER 13
BIG AGAIN

"Come in, Lin! Can you hear me?" I said into my Invisible Communicator, but it was no use. Lin wasn't listening. I tried to call Professor Penrod, but he didn't answer, either.

"Come on, Bruno. Let's go see if we can get their attention," I said. Bruno jumped up, wagged his tail, and ran to me, excited by the sound of my voice.

As he ran by, I grabbed on to his wide crest, swung on his back, gave him a nudge with my heels, and we were off! Bruno was heading in the wrong direction, so I pulled hard to the left, and he responded so fast it was as if we were sharing one mind. I had to admit, I was pretty proud of how much better I'd gotten at riding Bruno. The first time I'd tried it I felt like I was going to get bounced off with every step, but now it was as natural as running on my own, only SO much better.

A shadow in the grass, cast from the guitar-string rails of the Slide-A-Riffic, acted as our guide, and Bruno ran with all his might toward a small grove of trees between us and the landing zone. I could hear Lin and Professor Penrod before I could see them, but between Bruno's clumping feet and the whiz of the Slide-A-Riffic's pulley system, it was hard to tell if they were happy shouting or worried shouting.

I looked up and saw the bottom of the Slide-A-Riffic, with Lin leaning out over the front with a large grin on her face. I got a glimpse of Professor Penrod; he was wearing Lin's skateboard helmet, but nobody was holding on to the brakes.

Bruno didn't bother dodging around the trees, which is exactly what I was hoping for. He smashed into the trees, toppling them over with ease, just as Lin and Professor Penrod were soaring above us. The trees smashed to the ground, branches and leaves falling in a tangled mess right on the landing zone.

The Slide-A-Riffic zoomed so close over my head that I had to duck as Lin and Professor Penrod swooshed into the fallen tree branches. I had done everything I could think to do to try to slow down the Slide-A-Riffic, but in the last second, Lin jumped from the front of the basket to the back, grabbed on to the brake, and hung off the back of the Slide-A-Riffic until it came to a screeching halt.

Professor Penrod was launched from the basket, and he let out a big OOOF! as he landed in the pile of leaves. Lin jumped from the back of the Slide-A-Riffic and ran with Bruno and me to find the professor. I slipped from Bruno's back and joined Lin as we dug in the leaves for Professor Penrod. When we found him, the helmet was a little dinged up and his eyes were closed.

"Are you all right?" I asked, and a little smile spread across the professor's face.

"That was simply stunning. I've never had such a magnificent view of the Microterium."

He sat up, rubbing his chin and adjusting his jaw. Bruno was so excited to see the professor that he nudged his way into the group and started licking the top of Lin's helmet.

The professor looked at Lin. "When can we do it again?"

"Soon, but next time we'll go even faster!" Lin said.

"Oh, I believe that was fast enough," the professor said. "In fact, next time I'd like to volunteer for brake duty."

"You're just lucky Lin remembered there WAS a brake. I was worried there for a minute," I said.

"I knew all along. I just wasn't in a hurry to try it out," Lin said.

I pushed the hair out of my face and held out my hand to help Professor Penrod up. He took it, then as he stood he gave me a great big hug. I totally wasn't expecting it, and it was really nice after such a long and crazy couple of weeks. All the worried feelings, all the thoughts of messing things up, and even the feeling that I'd failed the professor, were squeezed right out of me.

"I've missed this place more than I can express. And it looks like even more visitors are coming to greet us. Prodigious!" he said as a large HOOOOONK-HOOOOOONK! sounded in the forest behind us.

"Now, let's go get a firsthand look at that new lab of ours," Professor Penrod said.

"And a look at the playpen as well. That's where Pizza and Cornelia are," Lin said.

"Most excellent. I can hardly contain my happiness. In fact—" the professor said before being interrupted by my buzzing phone.

A text message from my dad appeared on the screen.

"Um, the tour might have to wait. It's getting late, and my dad wants to know where I am," I said.

"I need to get going, too," Lin said. "It's bingo night at the Song household, and I'm first caller tonight."

"All right, then. Let's get this part in place and zip back to normal size. A tour can always wait, but nobody keeps bingo waiting," Professor Penrod said.

The professor and I worked on the machine while Lin wandered around the new lab. It didn't take long at all to replace the little valve, and in no time the Expand-O-Matic was ready to do its thing.

"I think we're ready to get you home," Professor Penrod said. "Only one problem. Where is Lin?"

"I don't know. But I can find her," I said as I tapped the Invisible Communicator in my ear. "Hey, Lin. Where are you?" I asked.

"I'm in the playpen with Pizza and Cornelia. Come say hello!" Lin said in my ear.

"Follow me," I said to Professor Penrod. "We need to introduce you to the twins."

I led the professor to the overlook window in the back of the Fruity Stars Lab 3.0. He leaned out first, and I heard him gasp as he saw Pizza and Cornelia for the first time in real life.

"They are magnificent! I've never seen their equal. Look at the strength in their tails, their back legs, their JAWS! They are simply stunning," he said.

"I couldn't agree more!" Lin shouted up, and the Invisible Communicator shook in my ear. I pressed it to turn it off before she shouted again. "I'm going to teach them to do tricks. I think it will give them something to do instead of chasing the other Microsaurs."

"That's an excellent idea, Lin," Professor Penrod said. "But what is that large ball they are snacking on?"

"Oh, that?" Lin said, proud as can be. "That's just my own special invention. It's a healthy and nutritious snack I made. I call them Microbites, but when we're shrunk down they don't seem that micro anymore, do they?"

I leaned out the window with Professor Penrod to get a look at how large the Microbite was compared to Lin and the twins. My hair rolled out of the window and reached all the way to the ground below.

"That is huge," I said. "But we really should get back. The Expand-O-Matic is ready."

"Aww. I wanted to stay for just a few more minutes, but if you let me do one last thing I'll be happy to leave," Lin said.

"What's that?" Professor Penrod asked.

"Can I climb up your hair and come in through the window, Danny?" Lin asked with a huge grin on her face.

"If you call me Rapunzel, I'll invite Vicky Van-Varbles to sing at your next birthday party," I said, then I started rolling up my hair before Lin could start climbing it.

"Aww, man, you're no fun," Lin said. "I'll meet you at the penny. Guess I'll have to walk like a boring person."

I lumbered to the penny, packing my hair, which was heavier than I ever imagined hair could be, while Professor Penrod warmed up the Expand-O-Matic. But that wasn't the only thing warming up. Lin and Professor Penrod were warming up their jokes and trying them out at my expense. The hair jokes continued for a solid five minutes as the Expand-O-Matic came up to temperature, and the three of us took turns expanding back to our normal size. But let me tell you, it all stopped being funny to me after I expanded back to normal size and my long hair came with me.

"It's NOT FUNNY!" I said to Lin and the professor, who were laughing so hard they could barely stand up as we made our way to the barn-lab.

"Oh, it is funny, Danny. Just not to you," Lin said.

"Why did this happen?" I asked Professor Penrod. "I thought things only grew back to their original size. This is NOT original size."

"I don't know, Danny. It's opened up new theories in my mind, but sometimes the mysteries of science are inexplicable. Even the most well-crafted hypothesis can end up

producing a false positive. The most simple and understood theorem can be debunked by anomalies. And even experiments that have been repeated thousands, even millions, of times can return negative, causing you to toss the blame onto complex chaos theories," the professor explained.

I nodded, my long hair rippling behind me. Lin looked at me with a confused look on her face.

"You understood all that?" she said.

"Yeah. He said science is messy. Isn't that right, Professor?" I said.

He passed a large pair of gardening shears to Lin and kept a large wire brush for himself. "I couldn't have said it better myself. Now, which of Lin's haircuts do you prefer?"

"You were right, Lin. Today has been a very lucky day," I said, then I closed my eyes as Lin came in for the CHOP!

Lin's house was on the way, so I walked her home before heading to mine. I had plenty of time to think about the day I'd just had. I'd learned a lot about science and things being a little unpredictable, but what I mostly learned was that asking for help was not only okay, it was really smart. Well, in most cases. Asking your best friend for help with a haircut, well, that wasn't the best idea I've ever had.

My dad was sitting on the porch, reading the sports section of the newspaper, when I got home. He smiled at me, then the look on his face turned from happy to really concerned.

"What in the world happened to your hair, Danny?" he asked.

"Well, Dad. You know that science is messy, right?" I said.

He folded up his paper and tucked it under his arm, then stood up and opened the door for me. "I sure do, and I can't wait to hear the rest of this story."

I could smell lasagna cooking in the oven, and I nearly passed out thinking about how wonderful it was going to taste. "It all started when Lin scarfed down an entire box of Fruity Stars cereal in almost five minutes."

"Wow. That might be some kind of record," my dad said.

I looked up at my dad and smiled.

It had been a long day, but something dawned on me just then. I had a great best friend, an amazing micro-paleontologist for a mentor, a Microterium full of Microsaurs to take care of, and the best dad on planet Earth. Then I realized that Lin's prediction from earlier in the day was true.

Today had been a lucky day. A very, very lucky day indeed.

A MESSAGE FROM PENROD

"Hello there, Danny. Do you notice anything different about me? Give up? I trimmed my mustache, of course.

"I wanted to send you and Lin a quick message to once again say thanks for your help.

I know it's been a rough couple of weeks, but I think we've all learned a great deal. These lessons will make us all stronger and improve the lives of the Microsaurs.

"Unfortunately, or fortunately depending on your point of view, I've been called away again. In all the hustle-and-bustle today, I neglected to mention that I had met someone who might be able to help us with the Microsaurs.

"Danny and Lin, I'd like you to meet Dr. Sheela Carlyle. She's a renowned paleobotanist, a

dinosaur plant specialist if you will, that I met on a dig site in China. She was quite surprised to find out about the Microsaurs, and she's joining up with me again on a new adventure in the red desert canyons of Southern Utah. Say hello, Dr. Sheela."

"Hello, Dr. Sheela."

"And she's funny to boot. My kind of adventuring partner, for sure. Anyway. I'll be back in a few days. A week at most, so once again I leave the Microterium in your capable hands.

"Oh, and I nearly forgot in all the excitement today. But I've introduced a new herd of Microsaurs into the Microterium. I placed them in the far back corner in an area I've been thinking of as the rolling, grassy plains, but I'm sure you'll think of a better name, Lin. They would love a visit from the two of you. Perhaps you could stop by soon and introduce yourselves to them. They are an interesting herd, because they have somewhat adopted a stray. A very large stray, however. He's an Apatosaurus named Wilson. You can't miss him; he might be the largest Microsaur in the Microterium.

"Well, I guess that's it for now. We'll see you again soon, and remember: Adventure awaits!"

FACTS ABOUT TYRANNOSAURUS REX

- The T. rex was big! HUGE, actually. Not only were they as long as a school bus, a full-grown *Tyrannosaurus rex* was taller than a basketball hoop and weighed nine tons! That's more than a full-grown African bull elephant!

- An adult *Tyrannosaurus rex* had over sixty teeth that were up to nine inches long, and they were made for ripping and gripping.

- If you think Pizza and Cornelia are growing fast now, just wait until they hit the age of fourteen. Scientists discovered that was the most rapid period of growth for Tyrannosaurus by studying the bones of lots of different-aged T. rexes. When they hit the age of fourteen, they could weigh up to 2,000 pounds. Four years later, a T. rex weighs more than 12,000 pounds. And that wasn't fat—it was pure muscle.

- Even though the *Tyrannosaurus rex* is known for its tiny arms, their two clawed arms were actually very strong. Their arms were about three feet long, and after studying the arm bones and spots where the muscles attached to the bones, scientists estimate that T. rex could lift around 430 pounds with each arm. Scientists also suggest that arm wrestling a Tyrannosaurus would be a very, VERY bad idea.

- In 1997 the Field Museum of Natural History in Chicago purchased a 90 percent–complete *Tyrannosaurus rex* fossil skeleton for 8.4 MILLION dollars! The dino skeleton, which is nicknamed Sue after its discoverer Sue Hendrickson, is still on display today.

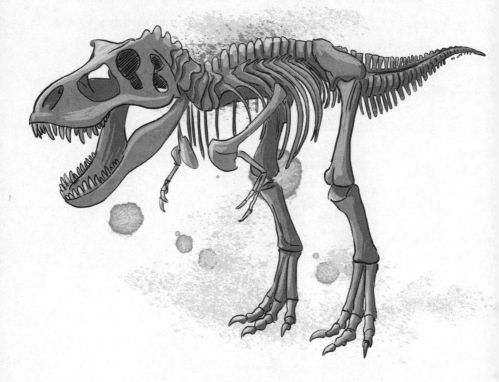

ACKNOWLEDGMENTS

This book, in many ways, echoes Danny and Lin's experience in the Microterium. It has truly been an adventure. At times, it has been an experiment. I would say there was a time there when it was a disaster. If I hadn't been surrounded by a team of VERY smart and supportive people, this book would have looked a whole lot like the Fruity Stars Lab 2.0.

So, I am lucky enough to have a little space to

thank those whom I relied on to make it through the mess.

My wife and constant reader, Jodi. The first line of defense. If she doesn't like it, it doesn't go out the door.

Gemma Cooper, my agent. Gemma gathers my complaints, my worries, my fears, and turns them into confidence. I have no idea how she does it, but I'm sure convinced it lies somewhere between magic and wonder.

Holly West, my editor. How did I get so lucky to find an editor who gets my Portal 2 references, introduces me to Critical Role, cosplays as my favorite Agents of Shield character, and loves dinosaurs? I mean seriously, HOW DID I GET SO LUCKY?

My children. Most of whom are taller than me now, and yet they are still not tired of hearing me daydream about Danny, Lin, and the Microsaurs. Don't worry, kids, I'm just getting started.

To the many wonderful people at Feiwel and Friends. Thanks for helping me achieve yet another crazy dream. You all hold a place in my heart.

And of course, to you, the reader. I mean—you are the best. You know that, right? Just the way you are. You are creative, smart, wise beyond your years, full of wonder, and ready for an adventure. I know because you obviously have wonderful taste in books.

DUSTIN HANSEN, author of *Game On!* and the Microsaurs series, was raised in rural Utah where he spent many days hiking red rock canyons that once belonged to the dinosaurs. After studying art at Snow College, Dustin began working in the video game industry, where he has been following his passions of art and writing for more than twenty years. When not writing or making video games, Dustin can often be found hiking with his family in the same canyons he grew up in, with a sketchbook in his pocket, a new idea in his mind, and a well-stocked backpack over his shoulders.

dustwrites.com

MICROSAURS

TINY-STEGO STAMPEDE

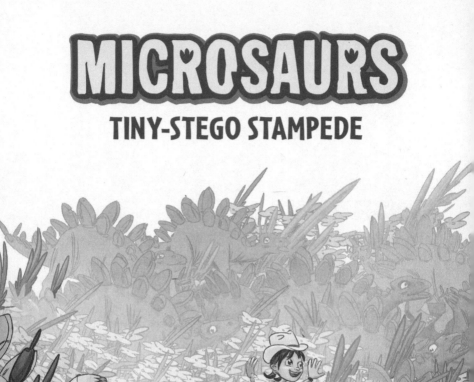

COMING JULY 2018